T0353848

The Adventures of
MICHAEL STEPHEN SKY

Michael Meets Mr. Bee

Written by M. S. Griffin

Table of Contents

Balboa Press books may be ordered through booksellers or by contacting:

Balboa Press
A Division of Hay House
1663 Liberty Drive
Bloomington, IN 47403
www.balboapress.com
844-682-1282

ISBN: 979-8-7652-5245-1 (sc)
979-8-7652-5246-8 (e)

Library of Congress Control Number: 2024909955

Print information available on the last page.

Balboa Press rev. date: 11/25/2024

BALBOA.PRESS
A DIVISION OF HAY HOUSE

The Adventures of
MICHAEL STEPHEN SKY

Michael Meets Mr. Bee

Edited by Sharon Oakes

EARTH'S CHILDREN

"Hey Michael!"

"Yes, Mr. Bee?"

"I want everyone reading your book for the first time to understand something important before they begin."

"What is it, Mr. Bee?"

"I want them to know that all the children on Earth must be protected, no matter what. It seems like humans might have forgotten how important that is. Children are your greatest treasure, and without them, there's no future for your species!"

"I agree, Mr. Bee! When I grow up, making sure all the children are safe will be one of my top priorities!"

"That's wonderful, Michael!"

As the sun began to set, three bright stars appeared above the summer horizon.

Michael Stephen Sky, a skinny, adventurous, ten-year-old boy knew, when the first three stars appeared, he had only thirty minutes of sunlight left.

"I must hurry!" Michael thought. **"This is the most important experiment I have ever done!"**

Running down the small, jagged hill behind his home in beautiful upstate New York; Michael was careful not to drop his fragile, glass jar.

Michaels face gleamed with excitement that early morning as he watched his mom carefully clean the family's last mayonnaise jar. In Michael's mind, having a thick glass jar with an aluminum lid made his jar special. Michael was looking forward to conducting his first floating water experiment with his special jar.

Inside the jar was the largest, yellow bumblebee Michael could find that afternoon. Never before had any bee lit up Michael's jar the way it was lit up today!

Michael has always loved and respected the many insects and small animals he discovered and observed in his family's garden. In fact, he would make friends with as many of them as he could. Why not? They were no threat to Michael or his family.

Observing them in their own world of movement was amazing to Michael. Michael learned early in his life, what improved his self-preservation for both now and in the future was good. What threatened his self-preservation was bad.

As Michael stared at his captured bee friend inside his clear, glass jar he thought...

"This big, yellow bee looks very different from other bees I have captured and set free in the past. This bee may have powers I don't understand! I have learned that power can either be used for good ... or for evil. I remember watching our evil neighbor destroy my mom's beautiful garden with his big, yellow bulldozer. I also remember my mom crying from the recent loss of our beloved President Kennedy. Evil comes in many forms. I must be very careful working with this big yellow bee!"

"AND NOW,"

Michael announced loudly, as if he was the circus ringmaster he heard on his family's black and white TV last night:

"I WILL CONDUCT ONE OF THE GREATEST EXPERIMENTS I HAVE EVER DONE! LIKE OTHER EXPERIMENTS I HAVE COMPLETED, I WILL PULL INFORMATION FROM THE INFORMATION MATRIX THAT SURROUNDS ALL OF US AND LEARN SOMETHING

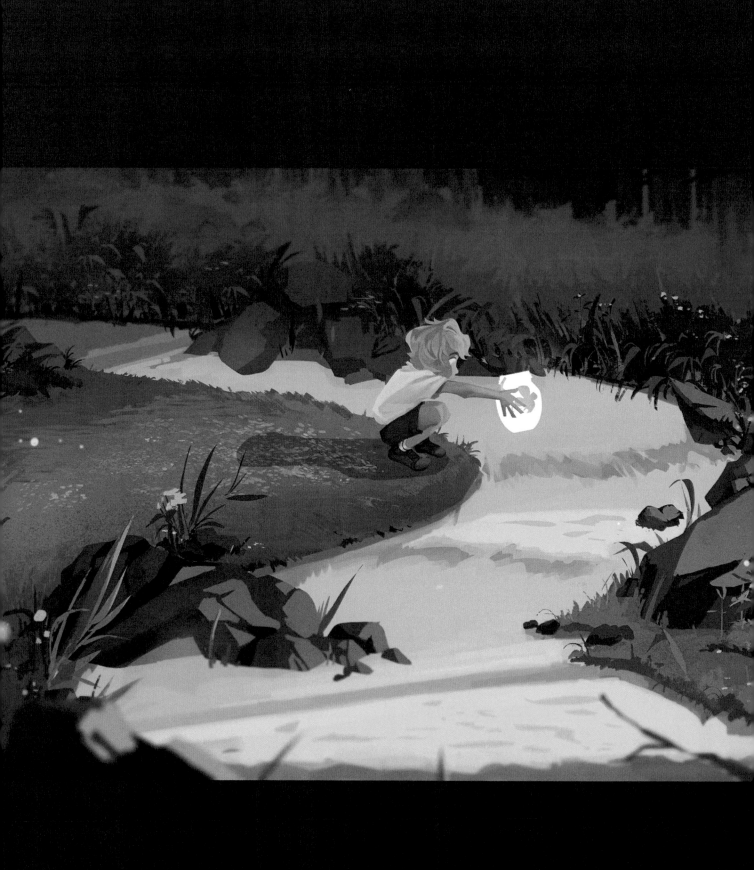

NEW AND TRUE THAT I WILL USE MANY TIMES THROUGHOUT MY LIFE! I WILL START BY PUTTING MY FAMILY'S LAST JAR IN THE BROOK BEHIND MY HOME! THEN I WILL FIND OUT IF THIS STRONG, INDEPENDENT BUMBLE BEE, IS ABLE TO FLY FREELY INSIDE THE JAR ... WHILE FLOATING DOWN THIS CONSTANTLY CHANGING BROOK!"

Feeling more confident—after making his first, loud neighborhood announcement—Michael ran to the edge of the brook and shook his jar a couple of times to make sure Mr. Bee was ok. As Michael held the jar over the water, Michael asked Mr. Bee, "Are you ready?"

Michael watched Mr. Bee lift off the bottom of his transparent mayonnaise jar, landing in a position forcing Michael to look straight into Mr. Bee's large, oval eyes. At that moment, Michael felt compassion for his temporary prisoner.

"Failure is not an option for us!" Michael thought, as he stared at Mr. Bee.

Mr. Bee (in his special way of sensing things) could sense and see the joy and excitement glimmering in Michael's eyes, as they both moved closer to completing Michael's water experiment together.

Focusing on the center of the brook, Michael carefully placed the jar, holding his new bee friend, on the water's gently... moving... surface.

"3, 2, 1!" Michael counted, as he lifted his hands slowly, releasing the jar to the control of the brook's unexplored and unknown destination.

Michael watched, with his eyes wide open, as Mr. Bee and his jar floated away.

The floating jar reminded Michael of the time that spring, he watched the mammoth energy of melting snow and heavy rains move the brook's water currents across the grassy lands into a new direction. That large change in the brook's movement was something Michael had never seen before.

"And now!" ... Michael thought. "Mr. Bee will travel in and be part of the brook's new path and new destination!"

Michael did not know where his jar and Mr. Bee would end up, if he let the jar float beyond the family's property line. If that happened, Michael may never see Mr. Bee or his jar again.

Michael's mom and dad both said, "Michael, do not go beyond the family property line! There are life-threatening dangers in the neighbor's dark, forbidden woods such as quicksand, big, vicious dogs and poisonous snakes."

Michael respected his parents and what they said, because his parents always showed high regard and respect for Michael. Michael did what his parents said to keep himself safe.

Michael thought to himself: "It is not the jar that is special—it is my bright, yellow bee friend who is special! I must run along the brook fast enough, so I don't lose them both in the fading twilight ... forever!"

Michael began running along the east bank of the brook, to catch up to Mr. Bee and his jar. As Michael ran faster and faster, he could see the big, bright, yellow bumblebee flying back and forth inside the jar.

Michael realized at that moment...

"My experiment is a success! Mr. Bee was able to fly back and forth inside the jar, while floating down the brook!"

Michael then shouted as loud as he could ... for all the bugs, small animals, and neighbors to hear....

"I LOVE LEARNING NEW THINGS!"

With that said, Michael had an amazing thought: "My bee friend is free to fly inside the jar, as it moves through the water, but my bee friend is not free to choose where the water will take him."

"So, what is freedom?" Michael asked himself. "Am I free ... or am I like Mr. Bee? I am free to walk around on the surface and inside planet Earth as it takes me on a ride through space, but am I free to choose where Earth's direction and future will take me?"

These were two questions most ten-year-old boys would not ask themselves, but Michael felt ok being different from other young boys he knew at school and in his neighborhood.

Michael continued chasing his jar downstream toward the family's property line. The property line was marked by a large, sharp, barbed wire fence, crossing over and above the brook's path.

Many of the fireflies, small animals and bugs who lived near the brook, heard Michael coming and quickly got out of his way!

Michael ran faster and faster, then splashed and splashed, into the brook's safe, shallow water—stopping the jar with one of his skinny legs!

"Wow!" Michael thought. "Being able to control my experiment is very important!"

"Thank goodness I stopped my jar and my bee friend from floating past the neighbor's barbed wire fence."

"What I learned today is ... I must not have too much control or too little control. I must have just the right amount of control when guiding my jar's direction and destination. With too much control or not enough control, I would have lost both my jar and Mr. Bee forever. Life is about discovering and applying the right amount of control to be successful. Only through practice, practice, practice, will I discover the right amount of control to be successful at whatever I choose to do."

Reaching into the cold water with his hands, Michael lifts the dripping, wet jar from the water, pulling it against his favorite brown shirt covering his chest. Squeezing the cap tightly with his strong hands, Michael removes the cap with ease. Michael watches Mr. Bee climb to the edge of the bottle's opening and stare directly into Michael's eyes.

After looking at each other for a moment, Mr. Bee communicates to Michael for the first time, using only his thoughts—saying…

"I am from the planet Zeglar."

"Wow, Mr. Bee! You can read my thoughts? I always thought you were a special kind of bee with your bright, yellow and white glow!"

"If you are still reading my thoughts Mr. Bee, thank you for sharing this successful experiment with me! This has been a very special day!" Michael thought.

"You're welcome, Michael! It has been a special day for me too. We will meet again one day in the future! My travels have taught me that our galaxy is full of many kinds of life forms including good and bad people. The good people are the most powerful spiritual beings. Their ability to create outweighs the creative ability of most other life forms. They are excellent at pulling new ideas out of the information matrix."

"Michael, I must tell you, the nature of my species is to measure the intent of all life forms either near or far away including artificial intelligence. Recognizing the intent of life forms is how we prevent them from harming us." Thought, Mr. Bee.

"Thank you for sharing that with me Mr. Bee. That sounds like a great defense system for your family. With that said, is there an abundance of life in our Milky Way galaxy much like what we find in Earth's oceans?"

"Yes, there is Michael! Our galaxy is teeming with all kinds of life. Each life form in our universe resonates with a different frequency thereby helping us identify each one as a friend or as the enemy. The first red flag the enemy shows is their use of deception to trick us. Their second red flag is when they try to dominate us. Their third and final red flag is when they move to destroy us. By knowing their intentions, we can avoid or stop them from reaching any of their red flags. The purpose of all life is expression! All life forms have the freewill to choose and express whatever they want including helping or destroying each other. However, each life form must choose wisely for whatever you choose ... will come back to you!"

"That is great information! I believe now ... is the time for you, the good and powerful Mr. Bee, to get back to your everyday life of being a traveling bee ... in our open galaxy! Is that correct Mr. Bee?" Michael thought.

"Yes, that is correct Michael." Thought, Mr. Bee.

"OK...SO...BE FREE! BE FREE!" Michael shouted for all the neighbors, small animals and bugs to hear! Michael watched Mr. Bee launch from the edge of his clear, glass jar. Mr. Bee

flew left ... then right ... toward the large, dark spaces in the neighbor's forbidden woods. Then Mr. Bee blasted straight up creating a loud POP sound! Mr. Bee's takeoff power pushed Michael's body back three steps! Michael watched in amazement, with his mouth wide open, as Mr. Bee ZOOMED up, and up, and up, in a wave of white lightning, heading toward the three brightest stars in the evening sky!

"Oh, my goodness!" Michael thought to himself.

"I have never seen or heard any bee ... Be so bright ... or ... Be so loud or ... Be so fast!"

Michael realized at that moment—Mr. Bee had been reading his intent and his thoughts from the very beginning, starting long before Michael put Mr. Bee in his jar.

"Wow!" Michael thought. *"What a wonderful, powerful bee!"*

As Mr. Bee's white streak faded beyond the dark horizon, Michael shouted for his new bee friend ... and for all Earth's creatures and people to hear:

"MAY THE MANY SPECKS OF STARLIGHT, GUIDE YOU ON YOUR FLIGHT...MR. BEE!"

At that moment, Michael discovered the answers to his two questions about freedom.

He thought: *"Mr. Bee, you have educated me! I can answer my two questions now!"*

"First, I am not as free as I want to be! I am stuck on planet Earth as it moves through space ... the same way Mr. Bee was stuck in my jar as it moved through the water."

"Second, I am not free to choose where Earth's direction and future will take me, unless I have choices. The more choices I have, the more freedom I have! Therefore, I will create a long list of choices found inside the universe's information matrix. All living beings use the information matrix that surrounds them, to discover new and better choices to make."

My choice list is:

"I choose to learn all I can about the many dangers around me, so I can work to overcome them."

"I choose to be wise, honest, trustworthy, and respect all life."

"I choose to work hard at being better, stronger and smarter."

"I choose to learn to fly many kinds of aircraft and spacecraft, so I too can one day fly up to the edge of Earth's atmosphere and launch toward those dark, forbidden spaces. Once there, I will overcome the life-threatening dangers of space travel and discover the many truths the universe offers as I fly among the brightest stars and most distant planets found in the evening sky!"

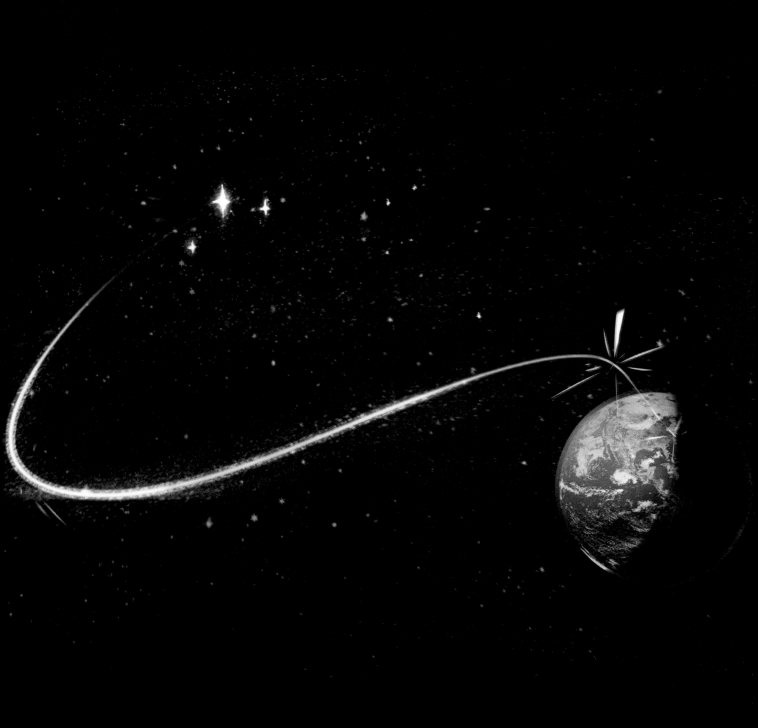

"I choose to come home from my space travels and share my knowledge and experiences to make Earth a better place."

"I choose to one day build a machine that will purge the information matrix to give people with good intent access to all knowledge in our galaxy and in the universe."

"I choose to defend, fight and overcome any evil that threatens me, our planet or threatens the individual freedom of the human race."

"So ... if you can still hear my thoughts Mr. Bee?"

"I too ... will use the many specks of starlight and truth to guide me on my fearless flights."

"I too ... will continue to be a seeker of adventure and a seeker of new knowledge!"

"I too ... will never stop being free ... just like you Mr. Bee."

"Just like you! ..."

THE END

INSIDE ALL OF US

We each have the choice to be or not to be,

the Michael Stephen Sky that exists inside all of us.

About the Author

M. S. Griffin is a debut author with a passion for aviation and philosophical exploration. A seasoned aviator, Griffin finds solace in flying sailplanes amidst the breathtaking mountains of Hawaii. Formerly a musician, his artistic background infuses his writing with a unique depth and perspective. Through his literary works, Griffin delves into life's big questions, guiding young readers on a journey of self-discovery and wonder. With each venture, Griffin embodies a spirit of curiosity and adventure, inspiring others to embrace the beauty of the unknown.

CONTACT INFORMATION

All illustrations were created by MaiChan.Creation

Our unpublished work was completed June 21, 2023

You can contact the Author at:
Michael.Stephen.Sky1@gmail.com

You can contact the Illustrator at:
maichancreation@hotmail.com

Or visit Michael Stephen Sky at:
www.balboapress.com

Mailing Address:
PO Box 372161 Honolulu, Hawaii 96837

Printed in the United States
by Baker & Taylor Publisher Services